His Love Brought Me Out

Cali Redbone

authorHOUSE

AuthorHouse™
1663 Liberty Drive
Bloomington, IN 47403
www.authorhouse.com
Phone: 833-262-8899

This is a work of fiction. All of the characters, names, incidents, organizations, and dialogue in this novel are either the products of the author's imagination or are used fictitiously.

Published by AuthorHouse 03/14/2022

ISBN: 978-1-6655-5403-9 (sc)
ISBN: 978-1-6655-5402-2 (e)

Library of Congress Control Number: 2022904305

Print information available on the last page.

This book is printed on acid-free paper.

CONTENTS

CHAPTER 1

THE BEGINNING

L et me tell you about me! A half breed girl born in Kansas City
KS to a Indian women from the three affiliated tribe, Mandan/
Hidasta/Arikara, and a father, a strong African American man from
Kansas City Kansas. I grew up and life changed for me after moving
to South Central LA. I grew up in the fast lane, I was told I was the
most beautiful creation, god has made it went, to my head. I looked
in the mirror and I told myself your new name is Cali Redbone sweet
pretty little thang, Coca Cola body shape, long wavy hair, caramel
red tone skin. Whenever I walked in a room all eyes on me men and
women would pause as I strutted past. It's 10:30 pm Friday night, I'm
on my way out to the Meow Club, a private club for pimps, players,
and hustlers, and call girls hung out there. Own by an ex-call girl
Madame Kat. I was going out to meet my sister there we have some
business to discuss, pulling up to the club, the phone rings, I look at
the phone its Madam Star as I look in the mirror putting on some
lip gloss, saying to myself I'll call you back tomorrow! Exiting the
car for the valet parking attendant I grab my coat out the backseat.
Walked to the door befor I could grab the door I see Charlie Mack,
now me and him go way back he sales some of the finest clothes, his
girls or boosters he says is that the beautiful Cali Red yes Mack its

me as we hug say a few words to each other, Mack says Cali I got a whole wardrobe for you I got your favorite Chanel, LV. I got it all here's my card call me in the morning as I head to the bar, looking around nothing but ballers in the V.I.P. Section, I get a seat at the bar, I see Ted the bartender, I'm so proud of him, he was a ex-junkie strung out on heroin. Madam Kat took him in as her son, Madam Kat is all alone she never had children when she was 20yr old she killed a trick who tried to rob her she grab his gun and it went off and shot him in the chest he died instantly. She did 15yrs in prison she got out of prison and got her self together parole and open up Club Meow. Sitting here vibing to that jazz it sounds so good. Ted come see me and said Cali my Redbone where have you've been? I just got back from Kansas City went to visit my dad and ended up buying a couple of fixer-upper so I stayed out there for a minute, I'm waiting on honey, what you want to drink? Patron and a slice of lime, OK I got you! Sitting there looking around, looking towards the door, I hear a voice say hey beautiful can I buy you a drink as I turn around to my right its a light skin brother standing their looking at me, with green eyes dressed to a tee, smelling so good, before I could open my mouth I can hear my sister way across the room hell naw! Dirty Red get your ass away from my sister, she don't won't no dealing with your ass, she got a mouth she can speak, I'm already taking knowing damn well I don't have a man. Laughing to myself! Honey walks over, looking at him all crazy, he laughs, and say Honey your ass ain't change, still crazy! Have a good evening ladies. Enjoy your evening and have fun! Cali Red I will see you around. I didn't tell him my name Honey as I hug my sister gurl. Cali don't mess with him he kidnaps women who he wants, I'll tell you all about his jive ass later, he ain't might type anyway I don't like pissed coloured, I like me some chocolate and baldhead tall brother. As the music play she takes off her coat, saying Aww shit that's my jam. Making her way to the dance floor. She loves dancing she second lines in N.O. dancing to the beat moving her body to the rhythm, here's Ted with my drink sorry it took so long, he bring an ice bucket with a bottle of Moet, Finess and said the gentleman in the corner sent this bottle to you as I looked over in the corner it's Slim, Big Frank and Charlie Mack as I nod my head saying thank you Slim is a pimp from northern California the bay area, big Frank is from Detroit he sales cars, sipping on my Patron, my phone beep its Madam Star texting me saying call me, so as I step down off the barstool feeling good that Patron got me ready for whatever, I join Honey on the dance floor dancing to the beat of grown folks music lights flashing Billy Boy blowing that saxophone Josh playing the drums a young papa singing his new song. Its getting late I tell Honey let's go get something to eat we go back to our seats to get us a drink, Ted says Honey what you having Patron on the Rocks, Cali a shot with a slice of lime please. Hey sis Slim sent us that bottle laughing, and telling Ted after we leave please return that bottle to Slim's table. Toasting to having the keys to Wiggles Inc. Honey we are going to have to make some changes on how the business is going to be ran. That motherfuckin D.A. won't let me have my freedom if he could take it away. We going to have to find a judge that can take him down. He thought the money he paid me, meant he own me. When we first met he fell in love with me he wanted me to stop working. I was in the game for 10years dated some of the richest men, ballers, lawyers, from all over the world. I accompanied them on ba-cations business meeting, player balls you name it. I got rich invested my money into real estate. So what now Cali? I got a plan I'm working on! What kind of plan? What mutherfucker would pillow talk yell that pillow talk! Phone ringing Hello mama yes Cali I'm doing fine did yea get the check I sent you yes baby I paid off the mansion; thank you so much the reason I called you is because I just got off the phone with Big Mama from N.O. She said she haves a friend name Mr Raw who needs a date for this weekend and she thought about you Cali, Mama you know I retired baby this ain't a regular date Raw is a wealthy man Mama I got my own money I know baby, he would be a good catch he is a perfect gentleman you can build a empire with him you never know. Also I need you to come by this week sometime and speak to the new girls. They heard so much about you and Honey OK Mama we will be there Okay baby I'll make you favorite Yakamen and

Honey some crab cake and crawfish pie baby I gave Raw your number Mama!! You should of asked me first, no baby I feel good about Raw OK see you this weekend, Cali be nice to him. I told him to handle you with care. Goodnight Mama as we pull up to the Pacific Coast Cafe. We get out our cars Honey steps out with her white mink coat and matching hat its cold, and Windy by the Beach. I grab my black fur coat out my back seat Honey says girl its freezing I grab her by her arm as we walked to the cafe entering, all eyes on us the waiter says ladies will it be table for two? Yes! Sistah I'm going to restroom that Patron hit me. Honey says you good, I wave my hand, walking towards the door entering, the stall to use the restroom, walking out to the sink, my head spinning. I put some water on my face and looked in the mirror and said Cali its your season, smiling patting my face, taking a deep breath, saying thank you Lord! for change. Opening the door walking to the table Honey says You good Cali Yes. I order your hot sausage samich and ice tea with lemon. Thank you befor I forget I talked to Madam Star she wants us to come talk to the new girls on Saturday Aww shit Cali I got plans but, I'll cancel anything for Mama. Honey do you know Raw from N.O.? Yes girl why? Madam set me up with him on a date, he just got out of that damn plantation you mean Angola yes the lp got him out and he got a big settlement and he invested in real estate, he use to be big time back in the days he owns alot of properties in the third ward and a few car lots, he's about 6feet tall brown skin handsome single rich. Well mama got a call from Madam saying he needs a date and he's a good catch are you going? Yes I think so. Well, what's our plan for Wiggle Inc? Let's look for some commercial buildings in Los Angeles we can open up a beauty supply and a cafe, what you think? We can call the realtor on Monday. Cali the reason why I didn't want you talking to Dirty Red is, he kidnaps women he wants; remember Mona Lisa she got involved with him and she have not been seen or heard from last time she seen her was about three months ago. Omg what you think happened to her I hate to say he might got her doped up somewhere, making money off her, she might be dead! I'll revenge her death his ass will pay, look after I come back from my date with

Raw. We must find her whereabout he dangerous Cali and so am I. I don't go know where with out little girl I rather get caught with it than without it! Waiter coming Ladies sorry it took so long, that's OK John, reading his name tag a young white boy blonde hair blue eyes, you have beautiful eyes sky blue well Thank you Ma'am no call me Cali, looking at my samich, looks delicious, thank you can't wait to bite into it, bowing our head Lord thank you for this food purify it and make it wholesome for the body bless the hands that prepared it. Amen. Waiter come back to the table and say's Ladies dessert on the house, OK wow thank you. Picking up my samich its nice and crispy how I like my roll biting down on it omg so delicious flavored too a tee fresh lettuce juicy tomatoes. Girl this samich almost taste like yours, love the way you make them. You ain't said a word girl you no me this samich takes me to my quiet place, I'm almost done how's your food Ima take it to go excuse me waiter I need a to go box, and I'll have a slice of red velvet and I'll have a chocolate brownie yes pack them cakes to go, and the bill as we get up to go pay the bill, honey see's a friend I recognize her, but can't place her, paying for the food, John walks pass handing him the change, for his tip wow thank you. Goodnight/Good morning John smiling its 2:12 am, Honey walks over do you remember her yes, kind of its Dimepiece remember she cut baby cakes face, ye'll I never liked that bitch, over 20$ I forgot about that, walking pass Dimepiece we make eye contact, she already know, I don't like her ass baby cake was young and was learning the game she looks with a stank stare Hey Cali I looked at her and kept walking she says you still mad at me, I turn around and said only dog's get mad! Walking out the door waiting on valet to bring our cars hugging my sistah as she alway pray for us, Honey love is a changed woman she the bestfriend, sistah girl god sent to me we both or the only child raised by single moms, but, we both know our father. OK call you in the morning. Getting in my car headed up the coast, tired full, sleepy. Breeze feels so good.

CHAPTER 2

TEN TOES DOWN

Its 3:15 am phoning ringing 504 area code looking at phone, it must be Raw hello, yes is this thee Cali Red this is she, this is Raw. Yes Madam Star gave me your number, I told her I need a date for a important business meeting, would you be so kind to accompany me sure why not OK I'll send a car to pick you, no don't bother I have my own driver, Oh OK Ms Cali, well kool your ticket will be at United Airlines desk, you don't have to bring nothing I got you Cali OK thank you, well I see you Saturday, your in for a treat, I can't wait goodnight see you soon! Hanging up the phone thinking to myself I sure hope this man is what I desire in a man good conversation and some good sex. Driving heading home listening to smooth jazz, wind blowing, mind wondering, Mama I'm going to take this last client, and I'm done! Almost home pulling up to my home reaching for the garage opener, opening the garage pulling in door closing reaching for my purse and coat stepping out Molly open house door to garge Cali Mija I missed you, hugging her, walk in house Alexa play my my jam. Walking threw the kitchen heading up the stairs you need anything no Mommie just my bed, I see you in the morning Yo Te Amo. Molly turn the alarm on please. Walking up stairs entering my room no place like home, taking my shoes off I break a nail o my thinking I got to get alot done for my trip walking to bathroom running bath water, pouring bubble bath smelling like roses in the water lighting candles diming the light, pouring a glass of red wine, take a sip looking in mirror saying Cali its all on you you have to come with your A-game N.O. men are straight forward, me down for whatever! Getting undressed to get in tub, I slide down in tub water warm feeling so good much needed. My phone beep text message from Raw Cali Madam Star said you are special, I smiled laying back relaxing the phone beeps once again Honey I made it home sistah. Laying back glazing at the stars threw the glass ceiling, I think about my mother Mama Bird tears start rolling down my eyes, nothing but good memories I could hear her say baby get you a country man, and never let no one change you, you got a good heart baby. Her sweet voice would alway say I love you Cali. Wipping my tears saying rest in pease my Queen, I cherish you forever, reaching for my glass of wine toasting to my Indian Queen til my last breath mama I love you. Sipping on the last of my wine closing my eyes relaxing in soothing rose scent, a evil thought just came to my mind about that dirty ass D.A. remembering him telling me while laying in bed with his cracker ass, him having to much to drink Cali, I put alot of drug dealers in jail who was innocent never knowing I would date they're kind of woman. You came in my life, that dirty son of bitch, thinking why he kept talking saying I'm going to be retiring in the next couple of years! You ain't going nowhere you can't go I own you. Our time together it was all about the money $20,000 transferred into my account from his overseas acct his wife knew nothing about, he said I will always be his well loved mistress, naw he was a trick and I was his special call girl I didn't like his ass, every other weekend for 8 years, I spent the weekend with him while he pretended to out of town on business I'll get his ass one way or another thinki Alexa play find your smile lathering my rag up to wash up thing gotcha!! I was taught what that really mean, that's mean fake love involved, by someone I thought really loved me, but as Honey sa I got you sis I believe her. Washing up imagining what my weeker would be like with Raw fantasizing!

7

I know once we chill he won't only want my company for the weekend, what will I wear to entice him? If he is what was described to me I'm in for a treat hope he can satisfy all of me mentally and getting out the tub wrapping up in a towel walk over to my bed, rubbing my body down with rose scented lotion, reach in my purse getting my strap out to put under my pillow, getting into bed it feels so good to be home in my own bed sleeping nude what I love doing! Falling fast asleep! As I sleep I dream. I dream of a man coming into my life to save me from my life style take me out of my pass into my future, I wake up sit up, and lay back down off to sweet rest, sweet dreams!

CHAPTER 3

PREPARING FOR BA-CATION

Waking up rolling over alarm clock going off it 8:35 am. Getting out the bed to start my day, phone ringing its Charlie Mack, hey morning Mack in running late give me 1 hour let's meet at Princess house, OK kool Cali I'll see you there. Opening the door Molly already have my cup of coffee good morning Mija morning Mommie, nothing like fresh brewed coffee, sipping on it going to the bathroom Alexa play my gospel play list. Getting ready to shower and start my busy day, screaming Hallelujah thank you Jesus for another day that was not promise yes Lord Hallelujah. Stepping into shower warm water running down my face, yes God new beginning, thank you worshiping my God, washing up, can't thank God enough for new mercy and grace! Steping out the shower grabbing towel looking in mirror thinking how God has kept me brushing my teeth, jamming to the music. Walking into my closet deciding what will I slip on to run out sweat suit and tennis will work sitting on my bed emotion running wild thinking of this man Raw, slipping on clothes. Grabbing my phone to call my hair stylish Precious phone ringing Hello gurl its Cali can you get me in today I need a touch up. Yes 2:00 open, I'll be there OK see you soon. Grabbing my purse and keys walking out the room going down the stairs, remembering I left my baby under my pillow don't want Molly changing my linen and see it. Run, back to room grabbing it putting in my purse Molly calling me Cali you want breakfast, that's OK got a hair appt, can you please get my luggage out of the guess room closet and bring it to my room I'm going for the weekend! Cali slow down Mija your always on the go! Business Mommie! Molly is my helper she's not a maid she's family she takes good care of me. Going to the garage to get in my car, opening the garage door I see a delivery man with flowers backing out, hello delivery for Ms Cali blowing horn for Molly, I asked the guy can I see that card passing it to me wondering who the hell knows my address? Its from that fuckin D.A. see you this weekend Cali my love. Molly takes the pink roses and say beauty, I'll put them in water, no throw them in the trash, Molly start speaking Spanish when ever she's upset she speaks her language. Pulling off heading to meet Mack, thinking about my busy day and my early flight in the morning phone ring its Honey. Sis I'm just getting up I'll meet you at the cafe in a hour. Thinking to myself you won't see me calling the D.A I know he won't answer this early he with his family phone ring one time straight to voicemail leaving message I'm still in Kansas, take care. Hanging up phone minute later my phone rings it the D.A. from now on when I see D.A calling that means don't answer! Pulling up Charlie Mack outside waiting. Hey Mack getting out the car walking over to his trunk. Wow you need to open a shop, I've been thinking about it Cali when I get off parole, don't need my P.O on my ass I got 6 more months to go. Looking at the clothes oh yes my size, what I owe you $3,500 walking back to my car to get my purse counting out the money. Passing it to him ain't you going to count it Cali you my girl I trust you! Opening my trunk Mack lays all the clothes in trunk. Thank you see you soon ake care and be safe. Phone ring its my daddy hey daddy how you I'm good baby just calling to tell you, they will be putting oday it both your houses, OK I'll transfer money to I still got the money you gave me. No dad I'll if you ever need something don't hesitate s his baby girl. OK see you soon love you driving threw my old neighborhood. I see little girls looking down at their phones when we was coming up we played redlight, greenlight, hopscotch, jax them was the good old dayz. I had a childhood I remeber when the street lights get to blinking before they came on everybody get to scrambling to their house see you tomorrow. It was dinner time bath time and bedtime these kids now days play on phones stay up all night, jumping on the freeway to meet my sister at cafe. DA calling that means don't answer, he leaves a message saying have your ass here Cali or I'm done! Yes what I always wanted to hear. Pulling into the cafe valet attendant standing hello Ms Cali, hey Mike detailer we be pulling in please take my car to the top level. Also Honey car when she get here. OK ma'am! Entering the cafe table for two. Please cup of hazel nut, phone beeping its D.A texting pick up phone delete his message and block him for ever calling me! Excuse this coffee is cold OK sorry I'll get you a fresh cup! Thank you, or you ready to order please give me a few minutes. Honey walking in they sistah with her country ass, kissing me on my forehead like she does always. Sorry I'm late, had to much Patron last night, how's your day going so far busy. I got a hair appointment at 2:00 I catch my flight to N.O. at 9:45 in the morning to go see Raw, so you ass going Yes, that's good you never no! Did you order now was waiting on you we can order now. Ladies can I take your order yes! I'll have the Belgian waffles and house potatoes scramble eggs and orange juice, and I'll have salmon croquettes, house potatoes grits wheat toast, apple juice, OK! I seen Charlie Mack I brought some clothes from him he said if you need anything call him. We going to have to get together when I get back in town, make sure you go by mama's tomorrow to meet the new girls, she knows I'm going on the trip, so we can shop when I get back, great I got a headache you want a B.C. powder, I got one yell. Omg love these waffle so delicious, Honey I really need this trip, haven't been with a strong black man in a minute, make sure mama get a girl for the D.A. I'm retired, I'm done dating after this one with Raw hell its not the money I need I need a Ba-cation, sex, gifts conversation, whining and dining! Eating the last of my waffles girl I got to get out of here, gone Cali I got the tab you need a ride to airport no, I'm good beside, your ass might over sleep, OK enjoy your trip love ya! Getting up going to the door walking looking to my right its one of my old tricks with his family as I walk past he stares making his woman look too! I strut pass thinking how I had to end it with him he wanted to leave his family a wife and 3 kids no way I was going to let that happen, walking out the door Mike gets my car, I just remember I forgot to tell Honey, that when I get back we got to find Monalisa, and deal with Dirty Redass thinking after this trip I got to go to Kansas again Daddy birthday coming up I'll surprise him with the deeds to the houses I brought and get him a truck he driving a old beat up truck now! Mike brings my car it is shining like new money, Mike thank you here you go little extra for the holiday, Cali thank you! Honey walks out Mike gets her car, pulling up who washed my car I had them detailed I needed it, ya herd me! Honey don't forget to take care of the D.A. We need a vacations, for like two weeks since I don't celebrate Thanksgiving we can go OK girl luv ya, getting in my car pulling off Its 1:30 heading over to shop to get hooked up by Precious, jumping on the freeway kinda of crowded phone ring its Raw. Answering How may I direct your call I'm looking for you, you good for your flight, yes your ticket will be at the desk United Airlines OK see you then! Thinking to myself I feel good about this date with Raw I'ma put it on him he will be so in love with Cali he can't live without me! Listening to slow jams daddy calls Cali I got the money, how's the carpet looking great my angel. I need you to find some tenants for both house for the 3 bedroom get a family with three kids rent $800 2 bedroom $600 daddy you handle everything I'll be down there soon love you got to get my hair done OK baby I love you! OK talk to you on Sunday. Daddy not knowing those or his houses. Pulling in parking lot I see my girl pulling in Princess, thank you for taking me in at the last minute girl. How's them babies getting big. Here let me help you, opening the door music playing fresh smell of cinnamon I love that smell. OK sit in the first booth I'll be right with you would you like some tea, coffee, or wine no I'm good. Just had a big breakfast. OK let me get set up be right with you phone ringing its the D.A.

Don't answer. Putting the cape on me OK Ms Cali let's do this, parting my hairs in fours she starts from the back, Cali do you know Mona Lisa Yes, well I seen her last week she was a hot mess she was with Dirty Redd girl Jewel they was at 7eleven, she looked at me and put her head down it was strange she didn't say nothing, she look like she was on drugs her hair was in two braids she had a old pair of jeans on. Tshirt and dirty ass tennis shoes on. Oh yell thinking to myself. Thank you Lord, thank you she's alive, not saying to much. Princess like to gossip. Texting Honey at shop Princess seen Mona Lisa she was with Dirty Redd's girl that bitch Jewel, she's alive sistah make sure you let mama know. We will handle that when we get back, in town sis get shit ready the vests and get Precious and lil Princess let them know we going in too get Mona Lisa love you! Princess I need a fill and pedi I got a big benefit I'm attending tomorrow need to be on point. OK I got you, door bell ring its my 3:00 client come, have a seat at the bowl I be right with you, she looks familiar that's one of Charlie Mack's girl Sunshine, Oh OK putting a cap on my head, Cali come sit under the dryer you want something to drink yell, I'll take a water. Sitting under the dryer thinking what will I wear, meeting Raw for breakfast in the morning once I land in N.O. got so much on Wiggles Inc. Mona Lisa, D.A. shaking my head to clear my thought, taking a deep breath drinking water. Princess says Chee Chee on her way to hook you up Cali. Watching Princess multitasking washing Sunshine hair putting her under the dryer. Come on Cali let me wash you, as I sit in the seat Sunshine looks at me and says Cali Red I wasn't sure that was you, I need your number I got what you like Charlie Mack is the connection, but I'm the one OK girl before I go I got you! Princess washing my hair rubbing my scalp it feels so good girl this red looking god, okay rinsing me and putting conditioner in my hair Cali sit here for 20 min. then I'll blow dry and flat iron you. Phone beeping its Madam Star Hello Mama yes Monlisa is alive she was with Jewel that trader ass broad, Mama I'll call you tonight I'm at the salon OK, love you too Cali be nice to Raw. I've been praying for you its time to settle down and give me grandchildren OK mama bye. Madam Star never gives up she haves to have the last word. Calling Molly, Mommie did you get my luggage out the guest room, si Cali si, tu mucho cansada, OK Mommie I'll see you and we will talk then. Cali Chee Chee is pulling in let me blow dry you and get you finish so I can get out of here I'm going to Cat Meow tonight, its the pre player ball, Cali you going oh no I'm going to N.O. in the morning I got a early flight. You enjoy yourself and don't drink to much, and don't take drink from strangers! Watch out you going in big girls territory alot of shit goes on, you ain't about that life. Thinking to myself she ain't ready, its some wolves in sheep clothes in there. Hey Chee Chee how you doing babygirl I'm fine Cali, I miss you, you must got someone else doing your nails, naw baby girl look here same set you did your the best babygirl, give me 20 minute to set up my station OK. Cali I need to cut your split ends hook your girl up! Thinking to myself I need to be right for Mr Right, he said I was in for a treat, naw he ain't knowing I am the treat, smiling Princess says Cali who is he you just smiling, no I was thinking about Honey, she say some of the craziest shit, OK you want eyelashes, no just arch.

OK Cali I ready when she finish with you. OK Cali look in the mirror, Oh shit you did that love the colour. Here you go thank you Cali this is too much, naw girl get you a offit look your best and be safe. OK you have a safe trip. Chee Chee I'm ready what colour would you like same clear with rhinestones. OK let's soak your feet while I hook your nails up. You want something to drink I'll take some red wine. So what have you been up too just working saving money to one day open my own shop. That's great when I get back from N.O. let's do lunch I got a plan. Me and Honey will be opening up some shops we got you. Omg Cali for real looking in her sky blue eyes looking like the ocean, she smiled Cali your the best! Here's your wine. Phone beeping its Raw hey beautiful my driver Pdiddy will pick you up in the morning can't wait to see you Cali. OK see you soon. Sipping on my wine my mind get to wondering what will this weekend be like no other weekend. Mr. D.A pops in my mind I know my mind must be playing tricks on me! Cause I'm done with his ass for real. Drinking the last of my wine. Thinking I'm ready for new beginning. Cali you like yes I only broke one nail this time putting on my tennis lol. Let's rinse your feet same thing yes. So or you going to Cat Meow oh no, that place ain't for me. Good stay away from their. I'm going to visit my NaNa. Give her a hug for me OK I will how is she doing she fine she broke a nail, you do right by her she loves you, do she still go to the same church yes faithfully I'ma have to visit her one Sunday. She would love that how's Jaylin and Lavell? Jaylin in college and Lavell live in Texas with Uncle Papa, yes I listen to his music I love that one song "Find Your Smile" we all get together two days before Thanksgiving at NaNa's house Uncle Leon home, and Uncle Billy, how's your Uncle Jay Jay he was over last week he just got married his wife is pregnant. OK sit over here so you feet can dry while I clean up, OK calling Molly Mommie did you cook yes Mija I made your favorite Pazole OK I'll be home in 30 minute, OK Cali sita. Chee Chee give this money to NaNa tell her it's my offering wow Cali. And here for you thank you Cali. Dig in my bag and get out a pair of sandles, these or beautiful I got 2 pair take one for you No Cali yes Chee Chee thank you. Putting sandles on feet looking beautif. standing up looking in mirror girl you show look good saying to myself. OK ready let me help you don't want you to break your nail walking to my car what kind of car is that Cali a Bentley, One day I'ma have a nice car you will baby girl! Getting into our cars pulling off waving heading home its 6:45 pm a few hours to sleep, need to pack. Hair blowing in the wind jamming to smooth jazz nice breeze sun setting, feeling good off that wine driving car smelling good the detailers always do a great job, smelling like strawberries, jumping on the freeway, not too crowded flowing phone ring looking down its my driver Deor Hello, Cal what time should I pick you up in the morning plane leave at 9:30 AM so 8:00 AM will work OK Cali see you then Deor did you get your enevolope at the house No Cali its been their for a week also can you take the Hummer for a tune up. OK see you in the morning! Pulling up to house opening the garage pulling in Molly standing at the door. She reaches for my bags. Walking in I can smell the pozole and tortias, wash up Cali and sit down, eat I'll run your bath and you eat bath sleep. Sitting down to a big bowl yes tasting the pozole so good thank you Mommie. Alexa play my playlist. Sitting at the dinning table chandelier sparling music playing enjoying this food to the last spoon full delicious, so full dumping what's left into garbage disposal. Cali I got go take your bath Mija. Turn the alarm on Mommie goodnight I'm leaving in the morning I'll be back in a couple of days the pool man will be here tomorrow to change filter, pay him with the card. Invite your kids and grandkids over have fun. Walking in my room I see flower Mommie! Mommie! What did I ask you to do with them damn flower I'm sorry they are so beautiful take them to your room please. OK! Shutting my door can't wait to get my clothes off getting undressed putting my bonnet on my head getting into the tub sliding down into warm lavender bubble bath rose scented candles burning laying back resting my head much needed looking up at the ceiling see the beautiful stars shinning bright. Dozing off shake it off washing up rubbing the loofah with suds all over my body. Getting up stepping into the shower to rinse off. Reaching for the towel feeling so fresh. Step to the sink, to brush my teeth looking in the mirror, seeing a woman with purpose saying to myself A.O.B. as I used to say back in the game. I am delivered from my past as of this day thank you Lord for watching over me. Walking to my bed grabbing my purse, getting lil girl out to put under my pillow, exhausted, dropping towel getting in bed I pack in the morning setting my alarm for 4am no place like home!

Goodnight World.

CHAPTER 4

THAT TIME HAVES ARRIVED

Alarm going of rolling over its 4am time to get up and pack. Getting out the bed stretching slept so good, walking to the bathroom to take shower Alexa play my gospel list, getting into shower turning water on thank you Lord for another day. Molly knocking on door Cali Cali your coffee Mommie use your key I'm in shower washing up, here's your coffee thank you Deor will be here at 7:00. Don't be late for your flight OK. Getting out shower wrapping towel around me. Looking in the mirror, smelling the freshed brewed hazel nut, sipping on coffee wake up Cali. Thinking to myself he said bring nothing I'll just pack a light bag thinking what shall I wear I'll put on some jeans and tshirt! No I wear a sweat suit and matching tennis (Gucci) putting on black thong and matching bra, grabbing some, lingerie, and hygiene and getting some money out the safe, grabbing lil girl from under my pillow to lock in safe Molly would be mad if she change the linen and see I carry a gun. Un wrapping hair, brushing my teeth, plugging in flat iron to touch up hair looking in mirror saying to myself Cali you will have a empire and help alot of family and friends. Molly screaming Cali driver is here, grabbing my bag coming down the stairs Mommie don't forget pool man. Will be here at 11:00 OK have fun Cali be safe Yes yo te amo, walking to car,

Deor opens door good morning Cali, good morning L.A.X sitting in the back seat texting Honey I'm leaving out. I'll be back soon remember to tell Madam Star to hook the D.A up with a nice girl. Text come in from Raw, can't wait to see you Ms Cali, likewise Raw on my way to airport, Deor please turn heat on. Not to much traffic great no luggage just a carry on. We are 40 minutes away. Relaxing listening to gospel, it helps me to want to be a better woman, closing my eyes worshipping and praising God. United Airline coming up Ma'am OK! We are here! Opening my door stepping out he passes me my bag. Thank you giving him a tip thank you Ma'am enjoy your flight walking into the airport its not crowded, heading to the desk, hello welcome to United how may I help you. Ticket for Cali Redd to N.O. OK let me see Cali OK here you or first class ticket enjoy your flight, thank you for chosing United.

Walking to the elevator waiting for elevator door open up its empty getting in pushing bottom to 2nd floor, exiting walking threw medal detector, hello the young lady says your hair is beautiful thank you, straight down threw tunnel boarding plane welcome right this way third seat Ma'am enjoy your flight. Well Raw knows first class for a queen. Great job! Ladies and Gentleman my name is Jesse Tolson I'm your pilot thank you for chosing United enjoy your flight we will be leaving in 15 minute. Looking out the window, Lord give me safe traveling grace. OK Ladies and Gentleman we are taking off this will be a six hour flight, Ma'am I'll have a glass of white wine, sure I'll be right back, here you go enjoy, sipping on the wine thinking this is a ba-cation much needed relaxation, some good sex and to be pampered by a man I choose to spend time with inhaling and exhaling finishing the last of my wine, asking the flight attendant can you please bring me a blanket, setting my alarm for two o'clock, starring out the window at the beautiful clouds feeling good, relaxed pulling the shade down turbulence plane shaking pilots come on intercom a little folks enjoy the rest of your flight. Closing my eyes drifting off. I can hear my mother sweet voice telling me she loves me and the sky is the limit Cali be all you can be baby. Missing her so much a tear roll down my face, MaMa rest no more pain my queen.

To be absent from the body is to be present with the Lord. Feeling so emotional and excited can't sleep. When I get to N.O I need a good meal, I should have let Molly make me some chorizo and eggs with homemade tortillas. I guess I'll turn on the T.V and watch a movie until I land, pretty lady is one of my favorite movies therefore inking to myself I'll be landing soon. It seem like I've been knowing this man already, laughing to myself, my mind ain't playing tricks on me this, is real what I'm feeling butterflies in my stomach. Maybe Madam Star, knows this is the man for me, she said no Cali you must go on this last date. N.O here I am getting ready to land the captain say we are now landing stay in you seats, and thank you for flying United Airlines. Plan shaking as we come to the stop slowing down, coming to a stop. Exiting the plan so glad I just brought a carry on bag only hate waiting for luggage. Its cold and windy here walking threw the tunnel walking threw the terminal not to crowded, exiting the building I see a guy with a sign that reads Welcome Cali Hello I'm Cali welcome to N.O I'm P.diddy your driver, opening the door there's a beautiful bouquet of roses long stem pink and a card that's says so glad you arrived. Driver pulls of heading towards the freeway, he ask me how was your flight it was nice thank you, where are you taking me driving toward a gated community, big beautiful homes, I'm taking you straight to Mr Row he's waiting for you at his home oh OK! We will be their in a few minutes. Arriving to this beautiful home he drives straight to the front door, in my mind wow, the big double doors open an older women comes out he parks, open my door grabs my bag I get my roses, the women says Welcome Mrs Cali welcome to Mr Raw home thank you Ma'am, no darling just call me Laura. Yes Mrs Laura no just Laura smiling as she greets me and take my roses, I'll put these in water for you. Walking in the door to the most beautiful home I've seen. Crystal chandeliers, sparkling the smell of southern food, just what I need a home cooked meal. As I walk down this long hallway afar I see a door, right this way Ms Cali Mr Raw awaits you. Entering the dinning area, I see this fine brown skin sexy ass baldheaded brother smiling at me with gold shinning with that smile looks like a giant to me. I'm only 5 foot 5 inches, hello sexy ass Cali Redbone, Madam Star said you was special smiling as I approach him I forget all about the food he hugs me and kiss my my neck his cologne drives me crazy I love his smell, thinking to myself welcome to my home, he helds me tight for a minute as if he was praying for me thinking in my head wow what a treat when he let me go he said you are so beautiful. Thank you I whispered. Thank you for coming, no thank you for the invite. As he pulls out the chair for me to be seated, please join me for breakfast, the doors open the servants come in with rolling tables many trays and varieties of breakfast food, smother potatoes, croquetts bacon, pork chops eggs grits you name it! Ms Laura says what would you like Ma'am I say No just Cali she winks at me remembering our conversation earlier. I'll have some grits croquettes, and potatoes, please so amazed Raw is stairing at me, he so handsome I can barely look at him without my flesh craving his body him sensing the attraction we both have for each other, biting into the croquet flavored, profectali mmmm. - so delicious, took a few bites, as I look Raw is eating his food so Cali how was your flight it was nice thank you I'm kinda of tired what time is your meeting later on great I have time to rest sure. He gets up walks over to me reaches for my hand as I get up he guides me out to a flight of stairs beautiful golden stairs with red carpet he leads me up the stairs to a room, as he open the doors never seen a room so beautiful room for a king and queen, where's the guest room he puts his finger to my lips hushing me I let him lead me he walks away shuts and locks the bedroom door thinking out loud Cali be careful what you asked for, coming back to me un zipping my jacket me take it off as he unbuttons his shirt, Lord all this chocolate for me, he picks me up, lays me on his bed pulling my pants down I couldn't say a word hoping he can tame me cause I've been needing this touch from a man who knows how to please a woman. As I roll over on my stomach I slowly crawl up the bed enticing him with my sexy carmel ass wearing a black lace thung he's standing there watching me as if I was the one he been waiting on he climbs in the bed as my heart starts to beat fast as he starts kissing my lips moving down to my neck as my body vibrates from his touch, he says damn Cali I've been waiting on you. Its about to go down in my mind Cali you better put it on him, and make him crave you. What pleasure I've been needing this I'm way overdue, he puts me to sleep after satisfying me.

CHAPTER 5

THE AFTERMATH!

Waking up forgetting where I was with this sexy ass man laying in bed next to me he's sleep just breathing I lay here staring at him he say's Cali why are you staring at me? He didn't open his eyes, I thought you were sleep, no Cali I was praying thanking God for my freedom I've was locked up in that plantation for 38 years. I knew when I got my freedom, I would find the women I often dreamed of and that woman is you, me! Yes Cali you. I couldn't say a word he opened his eyes beautiful brown eyes, looking over at me how do you know its me, I've been with other woman but never felt like this! I prayed that God would mold a woman just for me and then here you come! Awww so sweet Cali I really need a want you in my life, impossible Raw I live in Cali I got my whole life there friends family Cali we can travel back and forth here and there.

Raw I came to accompany you to this meeting on business, no Cali Madam Star told me you retired, so! You know what I did or was? Yes that's the pass I want to be you future we can build our empire together, wow I'm lost for words can I think about it! No Cali we were made for each other I want you in my life! Let's shower, and do some shopping he rolls over kisses me with so much passion and says I won't let another man have you. Walking into the bathroom his and her's everything shaking my head glass gold shower double headed showers as we enter running the water adjusting it just right. This handsome wealthy intelligent man, a man who prays and loves God he grabs me and pulls me close to him Cali we belong together, as we shower, look at me God allowed us to meet, at this time me coming out of prison you coming out of the game. We are destined for greatness, I brought a few things for you in the guest room, grabbing a towel walking out the shower opening the door leading to the guest room wow a room full of designer bags you name it Chanel, V.S. Sax, Louis Vuitton Versace. Get dress Cali I'll meet you down stairs kissing me on my cheek, I'm so emotional right now turning Raw how did you know my size well Madam Star sent me a picture of you and she also told me your size. Laughing to myself thank you Raw. Walked over to the bed grabbing the V.S bag panties, smell goods lotioning my body with my favorite, putting on a red bra seat thinking what shall I put on grabbing the Versace bag pulling out a suit I'll wear this matching shoes he know my size and style, thinking Lord what is you will give me a sign walking to the mirror combing my hair looking in mirror about to brush my teeth I'm so pleased, this man is a dream come true a man I could love and a man that would love me the way I always hoped and dreamed about. Looking like new money grabbing my purse walking out room looking at the bottom of the stairs there he is standing stairing up at me with the same exact offit on, see Cali we have so much in common, great pick I was hoping you pick that offit to put on great choice! As we walk to the garage this man have's a collection of cars, he walks over to a black Bentley opening the door for me no driver today Naw just me and you him walking around to the front of the car, looking so fine my mind get to thinking this man is the real deal, he made love to me like no other, as he gets in the car he reaches in his waist and says Cali I'm never going to get caught without it. Smiling as he gets ready to put it in his hide away box I say I hold that I feel naked without mine putting it in my purse. Looking around all his cars license plates reads Raw 1 Raw 2 Raw 3 Raw 4 opening the garage you like jazz sure we'll go to the French Quarters grab a meal exiting the mansion driving past the most beautiful homes, looking Raw says I need you to be My Queen to be complete smiling this is such a beautiful place.

I could get use to it. Wind blowing listening to slow jams, looking over thinking to myself he can love me like no other, pulling into the jewelry store, a valet attendant awaits us opening my door Hello Mr Raw good evening Ma'am No Ms Cali. He walks around reaches for my hand as we walk into the suite the jeweler say Hey Raw my friend come your room is waiting on you, when you called earlier I was on my way here. All eyes on us two woman whispering, I walk in with him taking a seat Raw whisper something to the jeweler walks out and a lady walks in with two glasses of wine passing me one I say thank you but, I'll take a empty glass with a fresh pour in my present, she looks in disbelief Raw says you heard her, as she leaves but I'm sorry baby they where whispering when we walked in so I don't trust them. The other lady walks in with a smirk on her face and says is their a problem Raw says my fiance wants a fresh glass of wine I look at him like omg did he say fiance!

Looking as she pours the wine saying congratulations Ma'am I said Nah I'm Cali Red. As the jeweler walks in with trays of diamond necklace and Rolex watches Raw says to me pick out a watch I laugh he seen I wasn't wearing a watch moving so fast I forgot to grab my watch from home. He was looking at the necklace let me see the one with the heart on it me looking at the variety of watches I think I like this one the jeweler Roheam says its new the oyster perpetual lady-date just 18ct features a white mother of pearl diamond set dial and a president bracelet yes I like this one. Raw says I need to use to restroom as he goes out I tell Roheam I want to surprise him with the man version here's my card wrap it up and put it in a box in my bag with my box and put my card in bag don't let him see its a surprise, as he returns picking up the diamond heart necklace he says a heart for a heart turns me around turning lifting my hair as he put the necklace on kissing my neck thank you Raw looking in the mirror so beautiful yes just like you. Roheim enters the room here's your boxes and bag warranties and cleaner winking his eye letting me know Raw's watch is inside the bag. Thank you both so much and congradualation I'll be looking for my invite to the big wedding and I like to design your rings! As we leave the two haters are standing at the glass casing. Me waving have a good evening ladies one smirking as I raise my hand diamond sparkling I actually wanted to through up Deuce but, I'll keep it sassy, and classy, valet attendant brings the car as Raw opens my door he such a gentleman loving this I could get use to him his love I feel for real, as he gets in car babe I'm ready to eat I crack a joke and say here in the car him smiling pulling a few blocks away. The restaurant sea food my favorite as we get out car the attendant greets us Good evening Mr Raw and misses, walking in the lavish place smiles all eyes on us 1 table for two indoor or outdoor inside will be fine thank you, waiter be right with you sitting across from this man who makes my liver quiver my soul happy, my flesh crawls when he touches me smh smiling Raw you are 1 and a million you make me feel so happy well! I aim to please you Cali and only you I mess with you the long way. What's the long way Raw. Baby trust is earned respect is given and loyalty is demonstrated a betrayal of any 1 of those and you lose all three wow that's deep baby when god made you he throw away the mold you are so different, yes God sat me down for a reason doing 38 years in prison made me who I am today I was wrongfully convicted. Almost 40 years but that's a conversation we will have one day. Good evening can I get you guys some drinks I'm Keisha I'll be your server. Yes I'll have a strawberry margarita and a glass of Patron with lemon please okay let me get that here some menus. Look Cali I've dated a few women since I've been home nothing serious no one got my attention like you do, what is it you desire in a women loyalty, and being true to whatever. You are the woman for me how do you know its me, my life is better with you than without you just the few days you've been here I feel complete. Also you retiring from what you did, you know how to take care of your man you know what it takes you survived, now I got you Cali. Keisha brings our drinks so refreshing, Cali excuse me I'ma step to the restroom to wash my hands OK! Waiter please bring me a empty plate with a top fast before he come back returning with plate I reach in my purse to get out the gift I got for him putting it on plate with two hearts love Cali. Here he come sitting down, what's this I'm not sure opening Oh wow picking up my note wow baby you got me you pulled this off matching Rolex. Thank you No thank you!

Picking up his drink let's toast to new beginning, and direction yes, sipping on margarita yes so good needed this! OK or you guys ready to order give us like 10 min please. Picking up his watch putting it on smiling what time is it me smiling your full of surprises Cali smiling at him sipping watching him drink that Patron alright don't drink to much I might take advantage of you. Okay you ready to order yes I'll have charred oyster and lobster with baked red potatoes with the works and lemonade. And you Sir I'll have a order of Cali Redbone Huh no he's kidding, I have lobster dirty rice and baked potatoe fully loaded and a Dr Pepper. OK I get this in and I'll bring you guys some breadsticks. Cali where's your phone I turned it off for the weekend you didn't have to do that I needed the rest free time me time us time, but I do have to call my dad tomorrow we talk every Sunday, where's your dad he lives in Kansas City. I'll be visiting him next month he turns 84 on Nov 18. I was just down their I brought two fixer upper I'm going to give him the deeds for his birthday and buy him a truck I love my dad I lost my mother June 22 I miss her so much she was my queen my sweet little Indian lady you have siblings, no I'm the only child, do you have kids no do you yes, one son, Cali you want kids yes maybe five when the time is right oh okay! Here's your food right here thank you looks delicious. Blessing the food Lord we thank you for this food bless the hands that prepared it. Amen. Dipping the lobster in the butter taking a bite, humm this is so good. How's your food Raw its good Cali can you cook of course, OK tomorrow you'll cook for me I got some business to take care of I'll be gone for a few hours can you cook for twelve people yes. What about the servants your the queen of my castle okay, few more bites and I'll be full, or you guys okay I'll have a glass of lemon water please. Cali you want to go listen to some jazz or go back to the house. We can go back to the house hoping you say that, waiter I'll take the check now. I'm going to the ladies room getting up walking toward the hallway leading to restroom walk in to wash my hands I look in the mirror looking at my diamond necklace so beautiful not only is my necklace shinning so am I glowing looking say to myself he is the one Mama I found that real country man you told me, that I needed in my life loving and caring drying my hands walk out the door and Raw is here standing waiting on me I grab him kissing his lips, as we turn to walk out Keisha says thank you for the tip you guys made my day.

Walking out its a little cold he wraps his arm around me as the car pull up he opens my door walks around gets in and says that food got me ready to relax driving wind blowing fresh air playing some slow jams heading back to the house, we can sleep till noon and Pdiddy can take you out to get your hair done and what ever else you need or you can drive yourself lil Diamond and he cousin Bre will be over tomorrow, pulling in garage waiting for him to open the door I get out he picks me up I'm so tickled can't stop laughing shorty your light like a feather carrying me to the elevator he steps in pushes the button put me down no I'll put you down when I get you where I want you door open to the bedroom he lays me on the bed untieing my shoes pulling them off removing my socks pulling my pants down, unzipping my jacket taking it off me laying there ready for whatever me laughing you crazy Raw yes crazy about you Cali Redbone! You need anything No! I want you to rest get some good rest baby, I got a few business calls to make I be back in shortly. So much on my mind looking at the ceiling thanking God for sweet rest Molly said I need to slow down. Laying here dozing off goodnight world.

CHAPTER 6

NEW BEGINNING

After sleeping well rested I'm waking by sweet soft lips good morning my Queen, I ran you some bath water I'm leaving out what time is it 6:30AM omg forgive me I was tired where did you sleep here next to you I watched you as you slept you looked so beautiful you didn't wake up til the king kissed your lips come bathe I got somethings to take care of Pdiddy got you Mrs Laura is here and Diamond and Bre, Mrs Laura grand daughter will be here. Walking towards the bathroom being guided by him the smell of roses and lavender undressing me, to get in tub please join me Raw as he undressed me drooling I let him sit down I sit in front of him laying back relaxing on his chest feeling so good Cali what we going to do, I need you here with me as he washes my back your life and my life will be so better as a team, Cali I won't take no for a answer I leave Monday Raw stay longer baby I've made the deal over the phone for the business meeting so, I brought some property in the 3. Ward and 9th Ward 4 lots I'm not sure what to do with them you can open up some business thinking to myself this man won't take no for a answer, I have to leave by Wednesday me and my honey my sistah we have business to care of how about you come visit me at my home. I would love that I will fly in Friday good so we got that taking care of let's just enjoy these next four days being with each other, Cali I'm in love with you, thinking to myself is this what real love feels like, the men I been with before was strickly business only. But this man here touches my soul turning to him looking him in his eyes I feel this love kissing his lips let's get out washing up as I stand up he is sitting the staring at me as I get out tub walking to the shower to rinse off I turn back and say yes, babe all this carmel belongs to you! Smiling as he gets out joining me in the shower and all this chocolate is your Cali kissing my neck Raw don't start I know I got alot to do today I'll see you at dinner babe.

As he rinses him sexy ass body off; walking to grab his towel looking back I left you something on the dresser, rising off walking to the mirror grabbing my robe looking in the mirror saying to myself his love brought me out. No more filthy hands touching my body. Walking into the guestroom to get something sexy to slip on, and there's a big gold box on the bed I open it, its a full length white mink coat I'm so amazed, I pull it out thinking to myself this man is the real deal I feel his love this is the love I need I could love this man like no other putting it on I was coming in here to get some lingerie, but this is even better he don't know I no about this beautiful gift taking it off to lotion my body with sweat sensations, to hypnotize this man love potions, laughing to my self as I put mink back on walking to the room before he leaves to get me a quicky since I went to sleep on him last night hurring up so he don't get dress to leave out I open the bedroom door he's in the closet I softly say his name he come out I'm standing there he looks wow you look fuckin beautiful you found your gift, walking slowly to him opening it up, dropping it to the ground he picks me up lays me on the bed. Me looking up at the ceiling saying thank you Lord for him my gift only god could of mold this man just for me his touch sends waves thru my body he knows how to please me my eyes rolling in my head moaning, with pleasure satisfying every part of my body Raw as I moan yes Cali stop please no its all mine say it say it call my name yes Raw its yours. Thinking Madam Star you was right me for him him for me, as we lay there breathing hard I take control him now calling my name, say my name Cali Cali will you be my wife, I need you in my life, I pause for a moment and say Raw this is how you feel in the moment, no stop it look at me I'm not letting you leave me without being mine I want you to be my wife Cali. So soon yes I know its you I want and need baby get you some rest before you start your day walking back into the bathroom to shower before he leaves I lay there thinking turning over dozing off ain't no place I rather be then here with him, falling back to sleep for a couple hours cause this man right here got that (whoopapeal). Waking up to a blue rose and two stacks of money note reads Cali here's some change to do what you need to do five thousand dollars ain't no change I love you Raw. Mrs Laura enters the room opening the drapes Good morning Ms Cali will you like breakfast in bed sure Raw gave me a order for you. Oh wow that man is so full of surprises. I'll be back in 15 minutes, thank you getting out the bed to take shower looking in the mirror I see sticky notes Will You Marry Me Ms Cali? Me smiling saying to myself I will be his wife. Getting in shower before my breakfast come, thinking this man is every woman dream come true. He is rich, sexy loveable, I could go on and on. Thank you Lord for blessing me with this perfect man who knows how to treat a real woman. Who is deserving of his love showering getting out, brushing my teeth looking in mirror I see a glow on my face happiness slipping on his robe smelling just like him, going back in the room so much to do today, thinking what will I cook breakfast is here thank you Mrs Laura, Cali Mr Raw is in love with you be good to him take care of him. I'll be retiring soon Oh no Mrs Laura he needs you, Cali if you say we need you I might stay long We need you OK child I'll stay thank you no thank you for making him happy he's like my son I love him, my grand daughters Briona and Diamond will be here soon if you need them to take you around, OK great can you tell P.diddy I'll be driving he can have this day off sure okay the girls will be here by noon its 10:46 now enjoy your breakfast thank you Maam opps Laura. Picking up to tip to my plate scramble eggs, green tomatoes grits wheat toast and fruit and coffee Raw haves me so energetic I can eat all this grabbing my phone to call Honey ringing no answer.

Dialing my dad ringing no answer thinking he must be plowing snow calling Madam Star ringing receiving text I'll call you back at Dr office. Eating my breakfast so delicious Turning on T.V. listening to some church this pastor caught my attention he said he who finds a wife finds a good thing and obtains favor from the Lord Proverb 18.22 Hallelujah praise God bless this man Lord.

Finishing up my food getting up to get dress thinking I put on some jeans and tshirt and some tennis to be comfortable got alot to do today slipping on clothes, putting on my necklace and watch, brushing my teeth, grabbing my purse putting the money in the drawer Raw gave me, walking out the room, walking down the stairs Good morning Mrs Cali beautiful day enjoy your day going into the kitchen to see what I'll need its been along time since I've cooked or went grocery shopping, wow what a big kitchen fully stocked Mrs Laura walks in and say's Mr Raw will be running late dinner will be at 7pm Cali I'm here to help you give me your menu and what you need, standing their with a notepad. OK I'm making garlic salmon baked fillet chicken breast OK we have both meats how many or you cooking for 12 OK got you, asparagus/sauteed Brussel sprouts red potatoes lime cilantro rice, we have garlic toast we have everything you need and a salad tomatoes cucumbers cherry tomatoes red onions. Bottles of red whine, white wine we can go to the wine cellar and get them, hello hello Mama where are you, that's Diamond, he baby hugging Ms Laura you must be the lucky lady Ms Cali Red well thank you. I'll ride with you OK walking to the garage thinking what car will I drive, walking that G wagon royal blue calls my name as I get in keys or already in ignition its like he knew I would drive this one starting it up ready to roll out, Diamond gets in taking selfie doing the thing with poking her lips out taking a picture I then realize this child done went live, its me Dimepiece and Ms Cali Redbone from Cali yall with her country voice phone ringing its my mother sister girl Brenda I call her B.B we been sistah for over 30 years we worked together before I got in the game, I missed her call I'll call her back later. OK Dime I don't have to go to the grocery store but, I need me some beignets and coffee to start my day OK Cali that's in the French Quarters!

Thinking I need to see Rohiem the jeweler I need to get Raw a ring we think alike we both or Sagittarius my birthday Dec 8 his Dec 17th so just incase he purpose to me I want to give him a ring a token of my love calling Rohiem, phone ringing Hello Cali Rohiem I need to come in and get Raw a gift I'll be their in 30 minutes OK we are closing at 2 today OK see you then don't tell Raw I called or come please oh no! I won't Cali you getting Raw a wedding ring no! With her little nosey ass listening to my conversation she might spoil my surprise just a birthday ring shorty oh OK! Thinking to myself the nerve of her, pulling up to get beignets Cali I'll get them for you I'm known here me laughing passing her money a long line she walks her little country ass to the front as she approach the front I see a young beautiful girl with red hair passing her a bag and a cup of coffee coming back to the car, getting in here you go. Who's that that's my cousin Bre I didn't know she worked the weekends here. OK pulling off all eyes on us stopping at the light a SUV pull on the side of us looking three woman looking start laughing, they think its Raw, Diamond roll down window Hey what's good oh I thought yall was somebody else Naw its me and Mrs Raw as we turn off they was surprise I think all the women in New Orleans probably know Raw. Pulling on Freeway heading to Rahiem's hey that's my song as the music plays her ass damn near dancing out her seat! Pulling up entering suite valet attendant Good afternoon Mrs Raw, walking in same to women at counter mouth drops when they see me, how can I help you, you can't Rahiem come out call come with me, walking in my private room how can I help you I need a ring with 38 Diamonds for Raw with my name ingraved okay pulling out three trays Cali this one hawes 27 this one 29 this one 35 I can add on if you find one you like I like this one OK its hush! Price doesn't matter how long will it take 1 hour OK I'll wait. OK looking at the time its 12:45 OK got time I'll call dad still no answer, calling Honey, phone ringing heffa call me I called you twice leaving message, Molly phone go straight to voicemail. Damn that's strange no one answering Honey calls missed called oh shit phone on vibrate forgot to turn it off. Diamond on her pone she walks over you good Cali yes shorty! OK I'ma be outside OK thing I walks up would you like some wine California Naw bitch don't play with me that's Cali Red or Mrs Raw to you looking at her someone done sliced her face already! Thing 2 said did she say what I think I heard ya heard me! Rahiem walks out Cali ready as thing 1 & 2 walks into another room. Looking at the ring so beautif sparkling I polished it passing him my card he passes me the receipt thank you Cali thank you I'm going to need you to design our rings soon yes!

Walking to the car Dime come Cali you ready yes I need my hair done I can do that what you want done flat iron I got you OK kool heading back to the house to cook. Driving pass the river I see family fishing kids playing I love the wind blowing fresh air Dime says Cali do you smoke I turn and look at her how old or you 22 girl I thought you was 16 I know I'm so tiny I get that alot laughing. Driving thinking if this man ask me to be his wife I'll be ready too, getting butterflies in my stomach just thinking of him, pulling in I'm so glad everything I need to cook is already here. Pdiddy washing cars Hello Diddy hey Cali you good yes sir. Getting out the car walking to elevator to go put purse up Dime stays there talking to her uncle. Freshen up a bit and get in kitchen walking to the room I see maids leaving for the day room smelling so good love the smell of pine soil walking into bathroom I see fresh flowers sent by Raw love you Cali Raw I love roses all blue long stem counting 38 roses wow!

CHAPTER 7

PREPARING!

Freshen up, ready to prep my meal walk into kitchen Mrs Laura haves everything out and ready. I gotcha Cali omg Laura please don't use that word gotcha I had someone tell me that and they did just what that word say got CHA! Mrs Laura laughing so tickled I've been their before I understand, OK I how about I'm here for you yes. Putting on a apron, rinsing the salmon in one sink leaving in strainer. Rinsing the chicken off in another strainer laying out four foil pans cutting up lemons, chopping up garlic black pepper kosher salt olive oil seasoning the salmon squeezing lemon it mixing salt and pepper in olive oil and butter together laying salmon in pans rubbing each one down with spices putting 10 pieces in each pan. Mr Laura comes in baby let me help you please its 4:00 honey I got this omg thank you. Get ready guess will arrive at 6:30, walking towards the door Cali your apron yes. Smiling walking up the stairs Lord bless Mrs Laura walking in the room its a dress bag on bed, I wonder who broughts this looking at beautif black dress with the back out drop dead gorgeous with some gold stilettos and silver one's two my God Mrs Laura did this I know she did putting my bonnet on my head taking of my jewelry putting it on dresser walking in restroom pulling shoes of jeans and tshirt, getting shampoo & conditioner ready to shower plugging in flat irons and blow dryer as I get in shower, thinking haven't check my phone had missed calls from everyone I call them later. Getting in shower pulling bonnet off to wash hair, getting in Lord thank you for this new beginning if its your will this man will ask me to be his wife, if its not Lord let us just spend the next two days together and go our seperate ways! Washing hair washing up rinse hair to condition phone ringing I'll get it when I get out rinsing hair turning water off steping out grabbing towel it Raw Hey babe I was showering how did you sleep baby you put me straight to sleep Mr Laura woke me up for breakfast thank you for the roses all 38 of them dinner cooking servants will be here at 6:00 to set table everything good OK see you in a little bit ok hey Cali I love you, for real! Hanging up phone, phone ring Cali you didn't say it back don't be scared I fuck with you the long way the right way, 10 guest is coming my son and his wife and Pdiddy and his wife Black Jeff his girl and a few others okay great bring that chocolate here, Cali you make my day. Turning on blowdryer drying my hair Dime knock on door Cali come in putting on robe sorry I'm late no you good blowdrying hair as I sit she takes over finishing OK its dry parting my hair she start flat ironing my hair I feel the heat girl don't burn me Cali I gotcha Oh no not that word again thinking to myself she's to young to understand! Please watch my ears I feel the heat. As she moves to the side of my head my nerves is running rapid precious is the only one who does my hair she's the best hair stylish in Cali. Alexa play my song by Valentino find your smile Aww Dime you got me looking good what time is 5:43 we or point thinking to myself this will be a special night I meet Raw son and friends jaming to the music Dime finishing up the front of my hair looking good Cali Hey that's my song deliver me Diamond says mine to as tears rolls down my eyes. Lord I need you today is the part that touches me looking back over my life times I was in a bad space, suicide crossed my mind just wanted to end it all but God step in when I lost my mother, my world was over but God said Cali you shall live and not die Hallelujah Cali you okay yes Dime God is good never forget that! Finished girl you hooked me up grab my purse off the bed, digging in my purse to pay Dime I give her two big face this is to much buy you something nice OK Cali enjoy your evening hope to see you before you go back to Cali so happy to meet you looks like your going to be around more Mama Laura was praying I heard her say Lord thank you for sending Cali into Raw's life! Aww that's so sweet thank you for sharing that. See you soon you are so amazing Lord thank you for keeping me and giving me the gift of love a man who loves you I know he is the one, Lord you washed all my sins away all the ugly memories of those different me touching my body, he doesn't even care about my pass, seasons come seasons go but, right now Lord I thank you its my season reaping season screaming Hallelujah. God you brought me from another state to love this man just want to say thank you. Looking at the time 1 hour guest will arriving.

CHAPTER 8

ITS THAT TIME

Cali Cali

It's me Mrs Laura everything is ready we set the table start getting ready okay, lotioning up Dime slayed my hair looking in mirror, putting on my diamond earrings and necklace, walk into bedroom I can hear Raw pulling in garage I miss him he haves been gone all day, let me put on these red panties set. Dropping the robe I know he will be getting on the elevator to come up I'll be the first sight he see door open I'm standing there he walks out grabbing me Damn Cali you look so good you know we got Quest, pulling in don't tease me baby, I need to freshen up so we can walk down together babe he take his shirt off, baby please don't tease me I'm need that lovin if you take your clothes off infront me laughing just kidding as he walks in the closet Cali what color black and gold baby looking threw his shirts to match me coming out closet with black slacks and a gold Versace shirt matching shoe baby look in that draw grab me some sock and underware I'm jump in shower OK baby can you zip my dress up. He walks over to me to zip me up I bend over to tie my shoe swaying side to side Cali your ass is so sexy laughing as I get up to let him zip my dress up he kisses my neck Baby your every man dream women, turning smiling phone rings its Brenda, picking it up Hey girl I called you two time I know I'm in New Orleans I tell you all about it send me a picture of you and him OK I'm on my way to dinner I'll call you tomorrow I promise! OK have a good evening Cali OK BB. Raw in the shower grabbing his ring putting it under my pillow I wont be needing a purse, grabbing his underwears and tshirt to set in bathroom. As he walks out Lord smh all that chocolate guest or pulling in Baby OK five minute I'll be ready. Sitting on the bed as I lace up my shoes, Raw walking out smelling O so good, slipping on his pants and shirt he sits on bed and say Cali my friends who I invited tonight or not just my friends they or family some have wives and some have woman friends they have heard me speak of you but tonight they will meet My Queen. Me grabbing his watch of dresser and his chain for him to put on we both get up and walk in bathroom to brush our teeth we smile we both think alike him at his sink me at mine as I look in mirror I see that glow on me I've never seen on my face happiness. Finishing up we both turn look at each other and he say's thank you Lord for my gift the woman you have molded for me my queen thee Cali Redbone! You ready kissing my lips.

CHAPTER 9

THE ENGAGEMENT DINNER!

What time is it 6:58 pm let do it, fixing his collar as we look at each other from head to toe, giving that OK he grabs my hand and we walk out the room walking to the staircase heading down the stairs, walking hand in hand reaching the bottom we walk down the hall toward the dinning room we enter all eyes on us all the gentleman stands up Raw says good evening this is My Queen Mrs Cali Red Hello everyone his son walks over to me and says Good evening I'm Miquel nice to meet you Mrs Cali likewise. All the women seated looking at me, from head to toe Hello I'm Troy Pdiddy wife and they all introduce them selves I see four empty seats, Raw walks me to my seat pulls out the chair for me to sit down and kisses my cheek. Walking to the dinning room closet opening out comes Honey, my daddy, Molly and Madam Star I get up so happy tears rolling down my face I then knew this was the special night, walking toward my family the ones who are important to me in my life, Honey screams out surprise I group hug them my Dad hugs me and say baby I'm sorry I didn't answer my phone me laughing hugging my daddy Molly Mi Amore Cali Yo Te amo. Madam Star See baby dreams do come true My little princess walking over to Raw you are so amazing thank you Thank you have made my day all day your are so full of surprises, as he says Cali you okay wiping my tears away as he pulls out the chairs for Honey Molley Madam Star he walks me to my seat once again, I call Mrs Laura over please go in the room under my pillow its a little gold box please get it and put it in your apron. Yes as she turn leaving the dinning area. Daddy says Baby or you okay Yes Daddy I'm just happy, Honey then say your ass ran away you know I'm coming for yo ya herd me! With her country ass.

Molly then say Mija you leaving me no Mommie your my family. Mrs Laura return winking her eye letting me know I got the ring, so if he purpose to me I'm ready. The servants come pouring wine, for the ladies D'Usse or Hennessy for the men, for some reason I believe its about to go down, Raw walk to me and says thank you for coming out to be with us on the special occasion all of you here are special and dear to me or either Cali, I like to say to Cali thank you for coming to N.O to spend time with me, I just want you to know as he digs in his pocket my ♥ beat fast Cali red I need you, will you be my wife omg Raw Yes yes, before you say yes Pops can I ask you to marry your beautiful Cali Yes Sir I won't have to worry about my baby girl no more, you have my blessing, then Honey ass say you got to share her laughing and I'm the wedding planner. Cali you said Yes and everybody else did to as he get down on his knee will you be my wife Yes he places a yellow canary diamond ring at least 5 carat so beautiful on my finger as we kiss everyone raises their glasses standing me saying wait a minute I have something to say Mrs Laura walks up to me passing me the gold box Raw looks and shake his head, Raw this here ring is a symbol of my love for you you are truly my gift from God this ring has 38 diamonds on it I know it represents time so I had this specially made for you I'm so happy you captivated me you make my heart skip a beat thank you baby as I place this ring on you finger you belong to me his eyes water Thank you cheers cheers to Mr and Mrs Raw a toast to our love baby let's eat and enjoy our family. Servants come out serving the food Raw says Cali prepared this meal for us. Smiling as we get served my daddy says I'll blessed the food this look delicious, Pdiddy wife say's yea going to have to give me the recipe I love garlic salmon sure you got me as a sister now

OK Daddy bless the food

> Father God we thank you for blessing us to all be together on this special occasion allowing us to witness this engagement between my daughter Cali Red and Mr Raw bless them in their union and bless this food and the servants in Jesus Name Amen

Mr Laura please join us your family.

As we eat Raw say's I got a winner my baby can cook she did this. Thank you winking at Mrs Laura. If I do say so myself it is delicious looking around everyone seems to well satisfied Raw enjoying his food the women or eating away, Daddy then say Honey you show no how to cook this salmon I never ate it like this, Raw announce, I want everyone to know we will be planning our wedding and I want to send all of you beautiful women on a vacation with Cali all expense paid and pops if you like to go you as well Oh no son, you made me travel I done got old I don't travel but, when you told me you wanted to ask me to marry my baby I had to come, she so deserving and I want a lot of grandkids Awww daddy your birthday is coming up, you need you a lady friend Oh no, I like being single after Chris died its just me and Jesus! Servant come in is anyone ready for dessert? Removing empty plates, we will be serving King cake, Red Velvet cake, beignets, coffee Mr Raw, the family room, or here, let's go by the pool room so I can whoop you on the pool table Raw laughing Miquel Cali do you know no one haves beaten my paw on his own table well as they say baby boy first time for everything I bet you $500 put your money where your mouth is getting up from the table all the men standed up ladies we all walk to the pool area If you guys want to make easy money put your bets in I know I can win Raw I got this we all laughing the men stay behind Mrs Laura can you bring a couple bottles of wine please! Sitting down taking off my heels Honey say Cali whoop that ass I hear the men coming Raw walks over to me kissing me and holding me can't wait for this night to be over I need to make love to you Cali, me smiling thinking about what he did to me last night. Rake them bets on the table Miquel give me my money now OK Mrs Cali, Pops you got this! As I bust them balls three falls in I have high balls you see that I got 4 balls left 9, 14, 13, 12 hitting 14 straight in, OK Cali the ladies cheering me on I stop looking at Raw you might don't get a turn aiming at 13, and 12 hit them down the middle they both go inside pocket Wow Pdiddy say Raw it don't look good, calling last ball pocket 9 straight in right pocket aiming hitting ball straight in Honey saying you got this Cali. 8 ball corner pocket aiming 8 ball straight. Raw is in disbelief what the hell me laughing pay the lady Miquel can't believe what just happen pops you don't even have a chance, Jeff Man Raw Cali is bad bad, $2500.00 on the table ladies each $500.00 for you guys turning looking to Raw I need you $11000 please sir digging in his pocket staring at me shaking his head passing me the money I give Honey another $500 and here you go! No Cali No I won for the ladies team Raw laughing Jeff's say's its getting late thank you for the invite Cali welcome to the family Jeff wife is very quiet she kind of look familiar, I didn't get your name Just call me New Orleans Okay with a smirk on her face, Honey steps in and say's is there a problem, no we good, Miquel said I'm leave to Pops Cali thank you for making my pops happy giving me a hug. Molly, Honey Madam Star we have guestroom awaiting you No we have hotel no you don't we have Bre go pick up everybodies luggage's and checked you out. Mrs Laura will show you to the rooms and I see you at breakfast should we say 9 am Goodnight I love you all so much Daddy your room is downstairs anything you need Mrs Laura number is on your nightstand Raw say's goodnight thank you all for coming. He reaches for my hand as we walk to the elevator, he say's you know you owe me for doing me like that right, I got you baby, reaching the room taking of my jewelry. Raw sits on the bed Cali you amazes me looking up say Lord thank you for my wife, my freedom, my salvation with new family, my children thank you with tears rolling down his eyes I walk over to him wiping his tears away Yes baby God heard our prayer

I prayed for the right man to come into my life and here we are we belong together. Untieing his shoes taking them off turning around him unzipping my dress as it falls to the grown I turn around pulling his pants off pushing him back climbing on top of him kissing his lips his neck his chest, as he flips me over he say's Naw Cali its all about you, thinking to myself this man no how to please me he kisses my neck licks my ear. Rolls me over kissing my back omg send chills threw my body, me moaning calling his name so satisfying, say you love me Cali, I love you Raw this night was so special you pulled it together thanks for my ring Cali you did that get you some rest my queen busy day tomorrow sweet dreams my love!

CHAPTER 10

TEAM RAW

Its morning can't believe I'm that special lady I'm his fiance looking at my beautiful ring dazzling and sparkling waking up to a note Baby I let you sleep, I'm going downstairs to have coffee with Pops I love you so much my future your king Raw looking at the clock, I need to get up Alexa play my gospel play list. Lord I thank you for a peaceful life, better days teach me to love this man correctly, let not my pass dictate my future, let me cater to his every need, let me be the wife his heart desire let me no the old Cali Red, never show up again I'm in a better place Lord thank you for change and a new beginning Hallelujah Lord bottle up my tears of joy and happiness. Yes deliver me Lord my jam, getting out the bed grabbing my robe, walking to tub Raw has ran my bath with blue rose petals leading to the tub looking at mirror he leaves sticky note Cali you've made my life so complete! Thank you, stepping into the tub water still warm sliding down so relaxing look up laying back Mama wish you were here to see me get married I have been lead by God that country man has found me the one you always talked about I need I'm going to give him children mom I miss you so much he has a servant she's like his mother she is so sweet wish you could meet here Mommie my heart cries for your loving caring touch I miss kissing your cotton soft cheeks rest mama love you til my last breath keep watch over me. Laying back relaxing got to get downstairs family will be at breakfast. Washing up love the sent of roses, stepping out to get in shower this song touches my soul Hallelujah, Lord deliver me. Showering all my pass wash it off me let it go down the drain this day, thank you Lord. Getting out feeling so refreshed walking in the room grabbing some underwear and jean and a raw tshirt to slip on a knock at the door its me Mrs Laura come in Cali good morning pulling the drape back Honey your family is here in the dining waiting on you, and I want you to know that woman that was with Jeff she and her family is into voodoo her sister liked Raw I knew she looked familiar she looks like one of them women at the jewelry store, thank you for telling me, baby no weapon form against you shall prosper. OK I'll see you at breakfast, getting dress thinking to myself she was shitty last night but God got me she will not be going on vacation with us. Brushing my teeth, putting my hair in bun. OK I'm ready. Walking out the smells of southern foods. Good morning family kissing Raw on his forehead and daddy on his cheek, Madam Stars say I need my Suga, kissing her cheek morning family how did everyone sleep wonderful, as I walk to my chair Raw gets up and pulls it out for me kissing the back of my neck. Daddy says I'm hungry let's pray father thank you for another day to be in the land of living with my family bless the hand that prepared it nourishment to our body in Jesus Name all say amen. Taking top off plate Mrs Laura knows what I like eggs grits salmon croquets wheat toast and fruit, Cali you like coffee No, I'll have a beer, just kidding water and lemon, Honey how did you sleep I didn't that woman with black Jeff had a hater face on her vibes was bad, but no weapon form against us shall prosper, Daddy then said she kept smiling at me Raw is that Jeff's wife No she his lady friend. She will not be going on vacation with us and it will be a secret where we go I'll be taking Pdiddy wife I love her spirit, Honey, Molly, Mrs Laura, Brenda, Diamond, Briona, Yo, Kadria, Chee Chee, Princess and Precious and Heaven. I am aware of her sister liking Raw, but greater is he that's in me/us than he that's in the world. Amen. So babe I was thinking we could barbaque out by the pool. You and the ladies can me and pops and Pdiddy going fishing Oh OK tell Diddy to drop Troy by hear, OK kool well since we are engaged family I will or should I say we will be living here and there, Honey I plan to have a summer wedding in Cali or New Orleans not sure we will figure it out! So I was think Jamaica, Dubai, Paris and Italy, Virgin Island, baby me and pops is going to get ready so you guys enjoy and Cali whatever you need I added you to my account your card on dresser Aww baby thank you, as he gets up enjoy yourself Daddy OK Baby I love you. Ladies what are we doing shopping out by the pool, or we could have spa day Mrs Laura no work for you, today Maria can take over spa day will be good excuse me let me catch Raw, getting up to catch raw before he pulls of Pdiddy wife is walking in Good morning beauty ladies in dinning area Baby what time you be in for dinner we are going to spa OK kool let's dine at 9 OK love, morning Diddy thank you for bringing the misses over have fun hope yall catch some fish. Carlos can you get the sprinter ready and have Rosa ready for a spa date she can drive us. Walking back an everyone bring or wear sandles Troy would like breakfast sure OK Maria bring her a plate. Sure Ms Cali what will you have Just some food OK laughing, I be ready in 15 minute. Meet you guys at the van going up stairs to get my purse leaving the card on dresser Raw know I have my own money treat on me today. Calling Raw! Baby I love you I waited to hear that coming from you my wife love you too enjoy your day see you later OK Babe, OK I'm ready Rosa pulls up to the front door all aboard Rosa your going with us to you have sandles no not with me well we can stop and get you, some Molly come on Mommie, Oh Callie Yo Te Amo Mi Amor. Love you too! Rosa the Ritz-Carlton spa. Rosa is my name I'm your driver seatbelts everyone, well be their in 40 minutes enjoy your ride ladies, Honey so what's been going on in Cali Well Mona Lisa is with Big Red, Precious called me and said she was there getting her hair did, was she her self? Was Big Red there no he dropped her off, was she in good spirits Yes she didn't have a phone and Big Red told her don't leave and he'll be back at 5:00. I was headed to airport Raw had called me he said he got my number from Madam Star so he flew us in girl you are luck lady he really love you Okay we will deal with Mona Lisa when we get back I'll have Bre and her crew kidnap his bottom bitch for exchange of Mona let's talk later. OK, Madam Star is sick Cali sick how she don't want us to know she have cancer you remember Susie the Nurse Yes she seen me at the outlet and said hey Honey I'm sorry about Madam Star I was like Huh she said You don't know she have colon cancer omg I didn't know please don't tell her I could loose my job Wow OK!

Sitting by Mrs Laura I want to thank you for everything you've done for me since I've been here and for taking me in Cali Raw never been so happy yesterday he was in the family room I heard him pray he was crying out to God telling him thank you for his wife and I heard him say teach me to love her correctly it touched me so I know he loves you. Mrs Laura do Diamond live with you Yes she stays at my house but, I stay here to run Raw's home, OK is your home paid for not yet well good I'm going to pay it off so you don't have to worry about that and when I travel you'll travel with No Cali no I insist! Okay we are here Mrs Raw, OK valet attendant Good morning ladies, this is Erica she will be assisting you, hello welcome to the Ritz Carlton I'll be your escort come right this way masseuse awaits you ladies enjoy. Can't wait to get all this tension out my back Honey says girl you need a man Cali shut up and don't wish that on me I'm OK with my "Eddie" OK. Ladies here robe you can undress in the room wrappin a towel around you and coming out that door to the deck and the tables await you thank you for chosing the Ritz-Carlton. Madam Star come by me I miss you so much OK Baby. Laying on bed, waiting Madam Star says Cali I need you and Honey to take over I'm getting old I want to retire Mama let the business go and retire and enjoy life. I'll give the girls all jobs we will figure it out baby the D.A been asking about you I told him you moved to Kansas with your daddy he said you blocked him I said just go on with his family he didn't want no other girl but, you Mama, Mama I'm not playing with him its over, I'm going to marry Raw and have a family and take care of you! And prepare for my wedding we can figure this all out let's enjoy this day today and live life too its fullest Mama I'm in love!

DEDICATION

I dedicate this book to Mr. Raw Ron Anthony Wiggins. He encouraged me to write this book and stayed on me about writing the book. It's a story about love, change, second chance, God is going to open them doors and set him free! My son Pa Pa who said right the book Mama Briona & Diamond my two daughter kept asking me Mom you finish yet so here it is enjoy this book! And my sistah Pam Taplin who's an author already who said you got this! Nothing is too hard with God!

To my son Leon Smith and William Swan and Joshua Swan. I know you will enjoy this book, and by the time I finish my next book you'll be home.

Mama, I did it, I wrote the book!

Cali Red Bone

Printed in the United States
by Baker & Taylor Publisher Services